-the-
PIRATE KIDS

The Very Quiet Parrot

BY Johanna Gohmann
ILLUSTRATED BY Jessika von Innerebner

Calico Kid

An Imprint of Magic Wagon
abdopublishing.com

For Charlie and Lola – You would make excellent pirates.
Sorry your parents are such squiffys. —JG

To CA who sings random thoughts with his ukulele.
Sometimes words alone are not enough! —JV

abdopublishing.com

Printed in the United States of America, North Mankato, Minnesota.
082017
012018

 THIS BOOK CONTAINS
RECYCLED MATERIALS

Written by Johanna Gohmann
Illustrated by Jessika von Innerebner
Edited by Heidi M.D. Elston
Art Directed by Candice Keimig

Publisher's Cataloging-in-Publication Data

Names: Gohmann, Johanna, author. | von Innerebner, Jessika, illustrator.
Title: The very quiet parrot / by Johanna Gohmann; illustrated by Jessika von Innerebner.
Description: Minneapolis, Minnesota : Magic Wagon, 2018. | Series: The pirate kids
Summary: Piper and Percy get a parrot for a pet. They try to get it to talk, but it's a very quiet parrot. They try to teach her to talk. They even offer her a pancake, but the bird still has nothing to say! When Percy is practicing piano, the parrot begins to sing. Their parrot loves music!
Identifiers: LCCN 2017946448 | ISBN 9781532130410 (lib.bdg.) | ISBN 9781532131011 (ebook) | ISBN 9781532131318 (Read-to-me ebook)
Subjects: LCSH: Pirates–Fiction–Juvenile fiction. | Brothers and sisters–Juvenile fiction. | Parrots–Fiction–Juvenile fiction. | Music–Juvenile fiction.
Classification: DDC [E]–dc23
LC record available at https://lccn.loc.gov/2017946448

Table of Contents

Chapter #1
A New Matey

Percy sleepily opens his eyes. His big sister, Piper, is standing over him. She is wearing her favorite pirate patch. The one with a purple skull.

"Wake up, brother," she says. "Mom and Dad have a surprise for us!"

Percy jumps out of his bunk bed.
He hurries to pull on his tall pirate
boots. The floor beneath him tilts,
and he almost falls over. "Whoooa!"

"Careful, silly!" Piper says. "We're
on rough seas today."

Percy glances out his round bedroom window. He can see the back of the family pirate ship. The sea is gray and foamy. He grins. He likes it when the ship is rocky.

Percy follows his sister up the rope ladder. Together they race into the galley.

"Argh! Good mornin', kiddies!" their dad shouts.

"Argh!" Piper and Percy call back.

Percy notices something big and round on the table. It's covered in a silky green cloth. "Is that the surprise?" he asks.

"It is! Would you like to see it?" their mom asks.

"Yes, please!" Piper and Percy jump up and down. Their mom slowly lifts the green cloth.

Piper and Percy gasp. There on the table sits a golden cage. Inside, a parrot with rainbow-colored feathers is perched on a small swing.

chapter #2
Finding a Name

"Shiver me timbers!" Piper squeals.

"Our very own parrot!" Percy claps.

Their dad smiles, then carefully

clicks open the cage. He sticks his

hand inside, and the parrot hops on.

"Parrots are incredibly smart. You can even teach her to talk!" their dad tells them.

"Hello, birdy bird!" Piper leans in to the parrot. The bird tilts her head to the side.

"She needs a better name than that," Percy says.

"Well, I'm the oldest. I should name her," Piper pouts.

"I'm seven, and you're eight. You're not that much older," Percy says.

"Why don't we name her together?" Piper suggests.

Suddenly, the parrot hops off her post and flies onto the counter. She lands on the toaster just as some toast pops up. She lets out a squawk of surprise. *Squawk!*

"That's it," Percy says. "We'll name her Poppy!"

"Poppy the parrot! That's perfect!" Piper laughs.

Chapter #3
Waiting and Waiting

Piper and Percy are sitting in the ship's crow's nest. It is Percy's favorite place to play. They are trying to teach Poppy to talk.

"Say, 'Hello, Piper!'" Piper calls to Poppy.

But Poppy doesn't make a sound. She just stares at them with her big eyes.

"Say, 'Poppy wants a pancake?'" Percy says, holding up a small bite of his breakfast. But Poppy still doesn't sa a word.

"Mom says she only eats seeds and insects," Piper says.

"I know. But we've been trying to get her to talk all morning. Nothing is working," Percy grumbles.

"Maybe she's shy?" Piper wonders.

"Maybe she doesn't like us," Percy mutters.

"No," Piper says. "We just need to be patient."

Percy frowns. It's almost time for
his piano lesson with Miss Melody.
He's worried he will miss Poppy's
first words.

A strong wind rustles Poppy's feathers, and she lets out a small squawk. *Squawk!*

The children freeze, waiting to see if she will say more.

Suddenly they hear their mom call from below. "Percy! Miss Melody has come aboard!"

Chapter #4
A Singsong Surprise

Miss Melody swoops into the music room. She's wearing her usual puffy, pink dress.

"Hello, children! My my, who is your new friend?" she asks.

"This is Poppy the parrot!" Piper says. She holds out her arm for Miss Melody to see.

"Well! Aren't you something!" Miss Melody sings the words to Poppy, and the bird flaps her wings.

"I think she likes you!" Percy says. "I like her too! Alright then, shall we begin your lesson?" Miss Melody stands next to the piano.

"Can Poppy and I stay and listen?"
Piper asks.

"Of course! That sounds fun,"
Miss Melody says.

Percy grins. He tries to slide onto
the piano bench, but it rolls slightly
away from him.

"My my, the seas are rough today!" Miss Melody pushes the piano bench back into place. "All right. Shall we begin?"

Percy peers at the sheet of music, then begins to play.

Piper sings along, "Yo ho ho! Come dance with me, matey! Yo ho ho! Come twirl with me, friend!"

Just then, Percy feels something sharp on his shoulders. Poppy has just landed on him! Surprised, he continues to pound at the keys.

Suddenly, there is a funny new voice singing.

"Yo ho ho! Come dance with me, matey! Yo ho ho! Come twirl with me, friend!"

Poppy is singing the song!

"It appears you have a musical bird!" Miss Melody laughs.

Poppy squawks out the end of the song, "Yo ho ho! Come dance with me, matey! Oh, a pirate's fun, well it never ends!"

The children and Miss Melody clap for Poppy.

Poppy warbles, then jumps onto the piano keys. She hops about, playing her own loud, silly song.

"My my, Poppy! You are lovely, but I think you may need some lessons, too!" Miss Melody says. The children laugh.

"Looks like I have a new piano partner!" Percy says.